The
Icicle Imps

First published in Great Britain by HarperCollins *Children's Books* 2011
HarperCollins *Children's Books* is a division of
HarperCollins*Publishers* Ltd,
77-85 Fulham Palace Road, Hammersmith, London W6 8JB

Visit us on the web at
www.harpercollins.co.uk

1

SOPHIE AND THE SHADOW WOODS : THE ICICLE IMPS
Text copyright © Linda Chapman and Lee Weatherly 2011
Illustrations © Katie Wood 2011

Linda Chapman and Lee Weatherly assert the moral right
to be identified as the authors of this work.

ISBN 978-0-00-741171-9
Printed and bound in England by
Clays Ltd, St Ives plc

Linda Chapman & Lee Weatherly

Sophie AND THE Shadow Woods

The Icicle Imps

Illustrated by Katie Wood

HarperCollins *Children's Books*

*To Alec and Callum Purcell for listening,
laughing and wanting more!*

Contents

The  Shadow Woods

Very few people ever enter the Shadow Woods. The crooked trees press closely together, their branches reaching out like skeletons' arms. Strange whispers echo through the quiet air, and eyes seem to watch from the shadows. Anyone who does go in soon leaves, their skin prickling with fear. For these woods are like no others. Hidden deep within them is a gateway to the Shadow Realm – a dark and chaotic world where all the mischief-making creatures like goblins, boggles and trolls live.

Many hundreds of years ago, the Shadow Realm

creatures could pass freely between our world and theirs, but they caused so much trouble that it was decided the gateway between the two worlds must be shut for good. Yet no one knew how to do this, until a locksmith with magical powers made an iron key and then slotted a gem from the Shadow Realm into its handle. The secret had been found! The locksmith forced as many shadow creatures as he could back into their own world and locked the gateway firmly behind them.

From that day on, the locksmith became the Guardian of the Gateway, watching over the precious key and stopping the few shadow creatures left in this world from causing too much trouble. As he grew old he passed his powers on to

his grandson, who in turn passed the powers on to his. For hundreds of years, the Guardianship has passed down from grandparent to grandchild, and the gate has always remained safely shut.

But now for the first time, disaster looms. The shadow creatures have stolen the iron key! Luckily, there was no gem in its handle when it was taken, but there are six gems from the Shadow Realm hidden somewhere in our world. If the shadow creatures find any of them, they'll be able to slot them into the key and open the gateway, letting hordes of villainous creatures loose to cause mayhem and trouble.

Only one girl stands in their way... and her name is Sophie Smith.

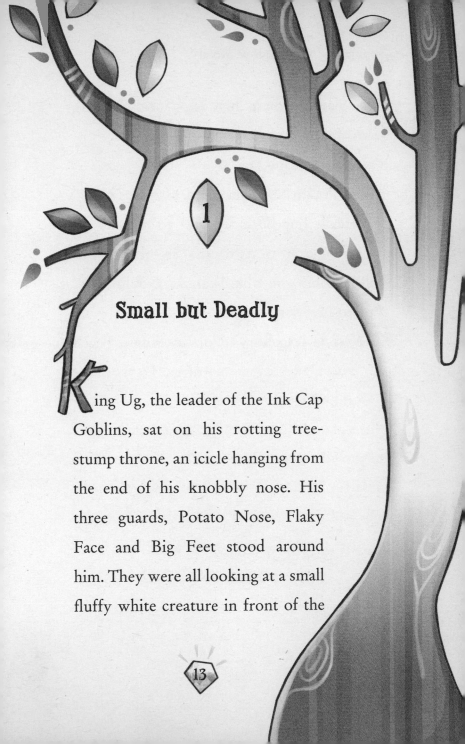

Small but Deadly

King Ug, the leader of the Ink Cap Goblins, sat on his rotting tree-stump throne, an icicle hanging from the end of his knobbly nose. His three guards, Potato Nose, Flaky Face and Big Feet stood around him. They were all looking at a small fluffy white creature in front of the throne. Standing on its hind legs, it bowed with a flourish.

"Greetings, King Ug."

"Aw," Potato Nose sniggered. "Isn't it sweet?"

The Icicle Imp bounded over to him, its left hand reaching up to its chest. "Sweet?" it spat. "Shall I remind you what I can do, Goblin?"

Potato Face turned pale. "Er…"

The Icicle Imp jumped on to Potato Face's foot. "Those who know us fear us! Do you fear me, Goblin?"

"I fear you! I fear you!" gasped Potato Face. "I'm sorry I said anything, sir!"

The Icicle Imp stared at him for a moment longer and then marched back over to King Ug who was chuckling. "So you want the Icicle Imps to help you find a shadow gem, King Ug?" it said.

King Ug nodded, pulling out an iron key that hung about his neck on a rope. "I have the key to the gateway here, but I need to put a shadow gem in the handle for it to work. The Guardian has already found four shadow gems. There are two left hidden around the town. Find me any single gem and the Icicle Imps shall be well rewarded!"

"It shall be done, King Ug!" declared the Icicle Imp. "We'll listen to the Guardian's conversations, we'll follow her footsteps, track her every move. As soon as we see her with a gem, we'll overpower her. After all, she's just a girl."

King Ug snorted sourly. "A girl who's beaten not only the Ink Cap Goblins, but also the Spider Gnomes, the Swamp Boggles and the Fog Boggarts."

"She shall not beat the Icicle Imps." The little creature drew his lips back.

The goblins caught their breath at what they saw.

"Excellent!" Ug chortled. "This time the Guardian shall be beaten. This time we will triumph!"

The other goblins joined in with his chortling, their laughter echoing up through the dark trees.

16

Sophie stood in her bedroom. She was still wearing her white tae kwon do uniform, and she had her long blonde hair tied back in a high ponytail. "Hands up… push off… bring knee around… kick," she muttered, going through one of the moves she had just been practising in class. Balancing lightly on the balls of her feet, she tried it at full speed. Bringing her knee around her body, she kicked out fast, but then she lost her balance and almost fell over.

She sighed and pushed her heavy fringe back. If there had been a shadow creature nearby

she was sure she could have done the move properly. Being the Guardian of the Gateway meant that whenever Sophie was close to a shadow creature her superpowers kicked in – she became super-fast and super-strong and could do all the difficult tae kwon do moves that she could normally only just watch.

Which was a good thing, because ever since Sophie's grandfather had told her she was the new Guardian, she'd met all sorts of horrible shadow creatures. So far, she and her best friend, Sam, had managed to always defeat them and now she had four shadow gems safely hidden in a purse belt that she wore around her waist. She and Sam were determined to find the two remaining gems before the shadow creatures did.

She readied herself in a fighting stance. "Watch out, flaky butt, here I come!" she muttered, picturing King Ug, leader of the Ink Cap Goblins.

Pushing off, she brought her leg around and kicked her foot out hard, imagining it knocking the king over. This time she did the move perfectly, landing without a single wobble, her fists up by her face.

"Yay!" she whooped, punching the air.

"You know, you are seriously weird!"

Sophie swung round. Her twin brother, Anthony was standing in the doorway. He looked like Sophie, with thick blonde hair and a tall, slim build, but his eyes were blue and cold, not green and friendly like Sophie's. He mimicked her, putting on a high silly voice. "Yay!"

Sophie frowned. "Go away."

Anthony rolled his eyes. "How did I end up with such a loser for a sister?"

"Get out of my room." Sophie spoke through gritted teeth.

Anthony deliberately took a step further into her bedroom. "No."

Sophie's temper snapped and she leapt at him, but as she did so she felt a familiar tingling surge through her. Her Guardian powers – there must be a shadow creature nearby! She didn't have time to stop herself. Her superstrength made her leap further than she had intended and she barrelled into Anthony. He flew backwards and crashed into the wall opposite.

Sophie scrambled to her feet. "I'm... I'm sorry, Anthony! Are you OK? Here." She tried to help him up, but he pushed her away, his face bright red with humiliation.

"Leave me alone, you freak!" he howled. Going to his bedroom, he slammed the door.

Sophie looked all around her. There was only one reason why she could be feeling like this. There had to be a shadow creature close by. But where?

Then she caught her breath. There, peering in at her bedroom window, was the small squashed-up face of what must be a shadow creature!

2

A Furry Spy

Sophie raced to her window, but before she got there whatever it was had vanished. She scanned the garden below. All she could see was the neatly trimmed lawn, the shed and the Shadow Woods beyond the fence. What was that thing? It had to be a shadow creature, but it had been so small! Hardly bigger than a squirrel. She decided to go and check the garden out and hurried on to the landing. But just as she did so, Mrs Benton, the housekeeper, came to the top of the stairs.

"Sophie, what are you doing still in your uniform?" she said. "Go and get changed."

"But, Mrs B—"

"No buts." Mrs B shook her grey head. "I haven't got time for extra washing this weekend. Not with the village fête tomorrow. Get changed, please, Sophie."

Sophie felt like stamping her foot. It was hard being the Guardian of the Gateway when you were also ten years old and expected to do as you were told. But she knew there was no point arguing with Mrs B. The housekeeper did all the cooking and cleaning and helped look after Sophie and Anthony. Their parents were archaeologists and often worked abroad, and when they went away, Mrs B took care of the twins along with their grandfather.

Running back into her bedroom, Sophie felt the tingling feeling fading – the shadow creature must have gone away. She slowed down and pulled on her jeans, a t-shirt and the black fishing waistcoat her grandfather had given her when she had first taken over as Guardian. Grandpa had been the Guardian before her and now he helped and advised her. She wished he was there, but he'd just gone out for his daily run. Sophie checked the clock. At least Sam was due to come around at any moment. She could tell him about the creature she'd seen.

She pulled out an old leather journal from under her bed. Tucking it into the deepest pocket

of the waistcoat, she went down to the kitchen. There was a delicious smell wafting from an array of cookies cooling on wire trays. Sophie reached out for a biscuit.

"Leave them alone," Mrs B said, bustling around. "They're for the fête tomorrow. Josie, Margaret, Marion and I are running the refreshments stall. You and Sam will help us, won't you, duckie? There'll be lots to do."

"Of course we'll help," said Sophie. The village fête was always fun. There was a pet show and a best blooms competition. "Are you going to enter Nigel in the pet show, Mrs B?"

"I'll be far too busy with the cakes." Mrs B went to a large cage in the corner. "Though I'm sure if Nigel was to enter, he'd win."

The grey parrot in the cage bobbed up and down on his perch. "In the bin!"

"No, I said win, not bin," Mrs B corrected him.

"Win. Bin. Win a bin!" cackled Nigel.

Sophie giggled. Nigel was staying with them while his owner was away on holiday. Sophie hoped that he'd never have to go home again. He was ace!

Anthony came in, a hopeful look on his face. Sophie waited for him to say something sarcastic

to her as usual, but instead he sidled up to the housekeeper. "Mrs B…" he began in a wheedling voice. "You know it's the pet show tomorrow and I've got some money saved… well, can I buy a pet? Just a hamster or something."

Mrs B shook her head. "I'm sorry, Anthony. No pets. That's the rule."

"But there's the old hamster cage in the garage and all my friends have got pets to take in the show and I haven't. It's not fair! I've wanted a pet for ages. Why can't I have one?"

"We're not having pets in the house," replied Mrs B.

"I'll get a rabbit and keep it outside then?" said Anthony quickly.

"No. You can enter Nigel in the competition if you want though." Mrs B went to the cage. "Come on, Nigel, say hello to Anthony."

Nigel screeched. "Hello, Pants-a-ninny!"

"No, no," Mrs B said hastily. "His name's Anthony."

"Pants-a-ninny! Pants-a-ninny!" cackled Nigel.

Sophie bit back a grin. Result! She and Sam had been teaching Nigel to say that for the last few days.

"Stupid bird!" Anthony stomped out. "I'm not entering him in the show! He'd be a total embarrassment."

There was a knock on the front door, and Sophie went to answer it. It was Sam, standing on the doorstep, wearing a coat and scarf and rubbing his arms. "Wow, it's freezing out here!"

Sophie stared out of the door. The puddles had ice forming on them, and there was frost on the grass. It hadn't been that cold when she'd gone to tae kwon do.

As soon as weird things happened now, she always thought about the shadow creatures. "Sam, I think we need to talk," she whispered uneasily. She saw Anthony watching them from the lounge. "I know it's cold, but let's go outside."

She grabbed her coat. "We're just going into the garden, Mrs B!" she called.

"What's up?" Sam demanded when they were safely away from the house and sheltering by the garden shed.

"This cold weather's really strange, isn't it?" Sophie said. "And just before you got here my powers kicked in and I saw something at my bedroom window. A little white creature. Do you think the shadow creatures could be out looking for a gem again?"

Sam frowned. "Maybe. There could be a type of shadow creature who can make it cold. Let's look in the Shadow Files."

Sophie took the leather journal out of her pocket. Over the years, all the different Guardians of the Gateway had kept notes about the shadow creatures they'd met, to help future Guardians. There were also clues to help each Guardian find the hidden gems. Each time a new Guardian took over, the gems magically shifted their hiding places. Then the old clues would fade and new clues would form.

Sophie and Sam turned over the yellowing pages. "Here, look at these Snow Goblins," Sam pointed out.

Sophie stared at the drawing of the squat goblin; it had spiky icy hair and big hands. She read a couple of faded words. "Brings snow wherever it goes. Hibernates in summer. Never seen between May and September. It can't be that then," she said, pointing at the words.

"There's another note here. Ice in summer? See page 65," Sam noticed.

Page 65 showed a tiny creature with big eyes, long white fur and a bushy tail. It looked a bit like a cross between a fluffy snowball and a chipmunk.

"It looks just like what I saw at my window!" hissed Sophie.

Sam read out the title. "Icicle Imps."

There were only a few notes alongside the drawing. "An Icicle Imp will bring freezing temperatures," read Sophie. There was an arrow pointing to its pointed ears and the words: excellent hearing. Another two arrows pointed to the imp's mouth and large dark eyes. BEWARE! read the label.

"Well, they don't exactly look frightening," commented Sam. "I reckon even I could fight one of those."

Sophie gasped as the tingling rushed through her again. "My Guardian powers!" Hearing a squeaking noise above them, she looked up and saw a white fluffy creature sitting on the shed roof! "Sam!" she exclaimed. "It's an Icicle Imp!"

The Icicle Imp streaked across the lawn towards the fence that circled the Shadow Woods. Sophie didn't stop to think twice. "After it!"

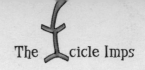

She and Sam charged after the ball of fluff. It dived under the fence and into the trees. Sophie could run incredibly fast with her Guardian powers, but she didn't want to leave Sam behind. Once they'd scrambled over the fence, she grabbed his hand and pulled him along as she raced after the flash of white, ducking under tree branches, leaping over roots.

The Icicle Imp finally stopped in a clearing and faced them, standing up on its hind legs. "Ha!" it declared in a high voice. "You have fallen into our trap, Guardian!"

Sophie bit back a smile. The little creature was about as scary as a kitten. "And what trap would that be?"

"Behold!" the Icicle Imp cried dramatically, sweeping one of his little arms around.

Icicle Imps popped into view on every branch

33

around the clearing. There must have been about
a hundred of them. But even so, Sophie couldn't
feel scared. What were they going to do? Cuddle

her to death? "Hey, Sam," she whispered, nudging him. "What did the Guardian say to the Icicle Imp?"

"What?"

She grinned. "S'nice to meet you!"

Sam snickered.

The leader of the Icicle Imps narrowed its eyes. "Guardian, it is time for you to be afraid," it squeaked. "Be very afraid."

There was a pause.

The leader looked at Sophie expectantly.

She cleared her throat. "Um, sorry," she said, spreading her hands. "But I'm kind of having problems with your general scariness. You're just so... so cute!"

"Cute?" the leader spat. He drew himself up to his full height of fifteen centimetres. "I warn you, we strike terror into the hearts of those who know us, Guardian!"

Sophie suppressed a laugh. "Yeah, if you're a dormouse, maybe!"

"Um, Soph," Sam said uneasily, as the Icicle Imps started to jump off the branches and move in around them. "They're getting quite close to us."

"So?" Sophie replied. "What are they going to do? Nibble us?"

As she spoke, each of the Icicle Imps drew back their lips, and a set of pointed fangs popped out of their gums – fangs that reached down their fluffy chins and looked as sharp as carving knives!

"Oh," said Sophie slowly.

"Attack!" squeaked the Icicle Imp leader.

"Run!" yelled Sam.

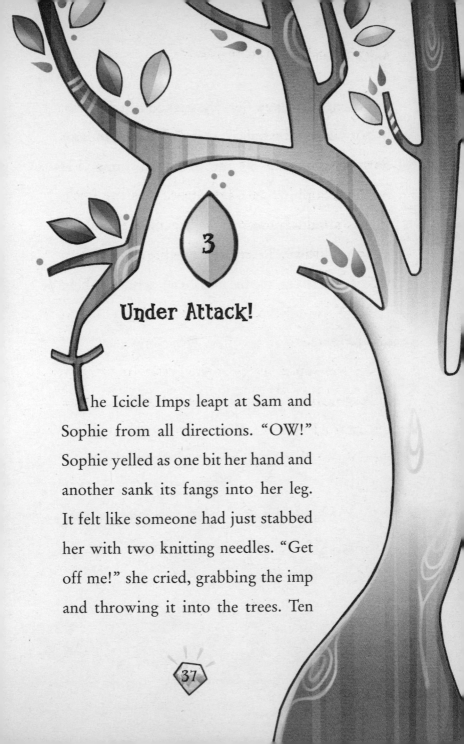

3

Under Attack!

he Icicle Imps leapt at Sam and
Sophie from all directions. "OW!"
Sophie yelled as one bit her hand and
another sank its fangs into her leg.
It felt like someone had just stabbed
her with two knitting needles. "Get
off me!" she cried, grabbing the imp
and throwing it into the trees. Ten

more imps attacked her. She kicked out at them, but although her kicks sent several of the imps flying through the air, more of them jumped at her head.

Sam shouted as an imp bit his ankle. Grabbing a branch off the floor, he waved it around him wildly, swatting at the imps and sending them

bouncing away like fanged tennis balls. It didn't seem to hurt them, though. They just landed, picked themselves up and leapt in again to attack, vampire-like teeth bared and little eyes gleaming.

Sophie advanced with kick after kick, but it was no use, they just kept coming back.

"It's like being attacked by piranhas!" yelled

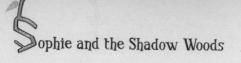

Sam. "Well, fluffy four-legged piranhas who aren't actually fish and who don't live in water and—"

"Sam! Shut up. Let's just get out of here!" gasped Sophie.

"Ha! I think not!" scoffed the Icicle Imp leader. He reached for his chest. To Sophie's horror, he pulled an icicle from his fur, and then another, throwing them like tiny lethal frozen arrows. With a yelp, she pulled Sam out of the way, but one hit her hand and blood spurted out.

"Let's go!" she yelled.

Together they charged at a group of Icicle Imps, thwacking out with Sam's branch and clearing a way through. Then, grabbing Sam and chucking him over her shoulder, Sophie ran at full pelt down the path and didn't stop until they reached her garden fence. They scrambled over it

and fell on to the icy grass. For a moment, they just lay there, panting.

"What's going on?" A voice cut anxiously through the air.

Sophie sat up and saw her grandfather jogging towards them in his running kit. He had short grey hair and was very fit. He had been the Guardian for many years before Sophie took over and he was the only other person in the world, apart from Sam, who knew about the shadow creatures.

Sophie groaned. She knew Grandpa wouldn't be pleased when he heard what just happened.

"Well?" he asked.

Sophie and Sam stood up and looked at each other. "We... um... we followed a shadow creature into the woods," Sophie admitted.

"You followed a shadow creature into the

woods!" Grandpa looked as if she'd just said she had decided to take a shark for a walk. "Why?"

"It was only little, Grandpa," Sophie said defensively. "It looked really cute and we didn't think it could hurt us."

"But Sophie!" Grandpa exclaimed. "Surely you know by now that you can't judge a shadow creature on its appearance alone? It was madness to follow it. You could have been badly hurt! What type of creature was it?"

"An Icicle Imp," Sophie answered.

"An Icicle Imp?" Grandpa echoed. "I'm not familiar with them. So, what happened?"

Sophie swallowed. "Well, we... er... we followed it and then it stopped and there were about a hundred more Icicle Imps in the woods waiting for us."

"They had fangs," put in Sam. "And they

threw icicles at us."

Grandpa looked alarmed. "Was either of you hurt?"

Sophie hastily covered the rip in her jeans, hoping Grandpa wouldn't see the deep cut in her leg in case it made him even more cross. "We got away," she said quickly, trying to pretend it had been no big deal. "We're perfectly all right apart from a few little bites and scratches. There's nothing to be worried about, Grandpa. Nothing at all."

The relief on Grandpa's face turned to a frown as he spotted her bleeding hand. "Nothing to be worried about? When the two of you clearly have sawdust for brains! You could have been seriously hurt. You absolutely must be more sensible! I can't watch over you every second of every day. Now, what do the Shadow Files say about Icicle Imps?"

Sophie took the book out of her pocket and found the page on Icicle Imps. "Not much."

"Let's see." Grandpa read the page and sighed. "Yes, well, you're right, there's not much to go on. Maybe you can add to the notes here after what just happened in the woods. You could write on the back of the page." He turned the

page. "Hang on." He frowned. "There's a clue for one of the missing gems here!" He held out the book incredulously.

Sophie read the words:

"'To find the diamond gem…

Where ponies and horses slept for the night

Look in a gable, the gem is in sight.'

"Oh," she said.

"'Oh'?" spluttered Grandpa. "I think this requires more than just 'oh'! So, you're telling me you didn't even check the pages on Icicle Imps properly before you went haring off into the woods!"

A voice carried down the garden. "Bob!" Mrs B was at the back door. "Would you mind giving me a hand, please? My friends are coming around later and I'm worried about the driveway being so icy. There are some bags of rock salt in the shed. Would you fetch one and spread some on the path so no one slips over?"

"No problem, Mrs B," Grandpa called back. He fixed Sophie with a look as frosty as the grass they were standing on. "You're really going to have to do better than this, Sophie." He handed Sam the Shadow Files then stomped away towards the shed.

"Whoops." Sophie bit her lip. "I don't think he's very pleased with me."

Sam looked at the page of the Shadow Files. "At least we've got another clue though. We'll be able to use it to find the diamond gem."

"What's a gable?" said Sophie, reading the clue over his shoulder.

"It's the triangular bit of a building where two sides of a sloping roof meet," Sam explained.

Sophie gave him a confused look.

"I'll show you." Sam dragged her to the old brick garage beside the house and took her around to the front of it where the two sides of the roof met in a point over the big blue garage door. There was a round porthole-like window beneath the point. "There!" He pointed up. "That bit between the edges of the roof, where the window is, is a gable."

Sophie's eyes widened. "If that's a gable then maybe the gem is in the garage!"

"No!" Sam shook his head. "Remember the first line of the clue? Horses don't sleep in your garage, do they?"

"Oh, yeah," Sophie realised. "Of course not."

Sam read the clue out from the beginning. "It says here: Where ponies and horses—"

"Shh!" Sophie stopped him hastily. "Let's go inside to read it. The Icicle Imps might come back and listen in. It'll be safer to talk in my room."

They hurried up to her bedroom, and with the door tightly shut they sat down on her floor and read the words from the Shadow Files out again. "OK, so it sounds like the clue's got to be in a place where horses and ponies live," Sam reasoned.

"How about we go to the local riding stables and see if that has a gabled roof?" suggested Sophie.

Sam nodded. "We could go after lunch."

"What if we come across any Icicle Imps on the way?" said Sophie.

Sam scratched his head. "There has to be a way to fight them. Wind dried out the Swamp Boggles and the Fog Boggarts dissolved in sunlight. What can fight ice? Of course!" he

exclaimed. "Heat! Heat melts ice. We could use fan heaters or hairdryers or something like that to blast them with hot air."

"We'd have to get the imps inside first." Sophie frowned. "Those things need electricity."

"Lunchtime everyone!" Mrs B called from downstairs.

"OK, after lunch, we go to the stables and on the way we plan some more," said Sophie. "Deal?"

"Deal," Sam nodded, and jumping to their feet, they ran downstairs.

When they had finished eating lunch they told Mrs B they were going to go for a walk. "Have you got scarves and gloves?" she fussed. "It's so cold outside today. I've never known weather like it in June. I really hope it warms up before the fête tomorrow." She insisted on Sophie and Sam taking a flask of hot chocolate with them in a rucksack.

When she finally let them go, they set off down the driveway. The trees and plants were thick with frost and icicles were hanging from fences and lampposts. "It's like it's winter," said Sophie.

Sam grinned. "I've got a wintry joke! What does Jack Frost eat for breakfast?"

"What?" asked Sophie.

"Frosties!"

Sophie chuckled. "OK. I've got one too. Knock knock."

"Who's there?"

"Icy."

"Icy who?"

"I see a..." She gasped and broke off from the

joke. "I see an Icicle Imp up ahead!"

It was true. A little way further on, an Icicle Imp was sitting on the fence watching them!

4

Icicle Imps Everywhere!

he Icicle Imp saw Sophie and Sam
staring at it, and disappeared into the
undergrowth in a flurry of white fur.

"Do you think it was spying on
us?" asked Sophie.

"Maybe," said Sam uneasily.
"Where's it gone?"

Sophie glanced behind them. She

was sure she caught sight of another little set of white tufted ears ducking behind a tree. "There are definitely more of them. This isn't good. Should we go back?"

"No way," Sam whispered. "We need to look for this gem."

"OK, well, let's get to the stables as fast as we can." Sophie wished she could use her superspeed, but she didn't dare. Someone might see them. They hurried on down the road and past the playing field where the fête was going to be held the next day.

Sam and Sophie cut down a bridle path that led to the stables. "What are we going to say to the owners?" Sam asked, as they approached the gate. "We can't just ask if we can check in all their stables."

Sophie wracked her brains. How would they

be able to get a look around without someone asking what they were up to?

"Hi, Sophie!"

Sophie saw Daisy, one of the girls in their class at school, walking down the yard towards them. "What are you two doing here?" Daisy asked curiously. "Have you come for a riding lesson?"

"We were just out for a walk," said Sam. "Have you got a pony, Daisy?"

"Yes, he's called Blue. Would you like to come and see him?"

"Oh, yes, please!" Sophie replied.

"Could we have a look around too?" asked Sam innocently.

"Of course," Daisy answered. "I'll give you the guided tour."

Sophie and Sam exchanged delighted looks.

Daisy led them up to a stable where a grey

pony was looking out. "This is Blue," she said.

Sophie and Sam were more interested in looking at Blue's stable than at the pony. Sophie was disappointed to see it was a modern stable with a flat roof and no gable at all.

"Come in and say hello." Daisy opened the stable door. Sophie stroked Blue's silky nose. He nuzzled her and then went to his wooden manger built into one of the corners of his stable, licking at his empty plastic feed bowl before looking hopefully around at them.

Sophie laughed. "I think he's trying to tell us something!"

"Oh, he's always hungry," said Daisy with a grin.

Half an hour later, Daisy had shown them the rest of the yard, but none of the stables had a gabled roof.

"Well… thanks for showing us around, Daisy," Sophie sighed as they went to the gate.

"Are you two going to the fête tomorrow?" asked Daisy.

"Yes," said Sophie. "How about you?"

Daisy nodded. "Blue's giving pony rides. I'll see you there!"

Sophie felt very disappointed as she and Sam trudged home again. She'd been so sure that the gem would be at the stables! "What are we going to do now?" she said.

"I dunno." Sam glanced at her rucksack. "Have some hot chocolate?"

"Good plan!" said Sophie with a grin.

They got the flask out, but just as they started to unscrew the lid, Sophie felt a tingle run across her skin. Looking around, she caught sight of an Icicle Imp peering from behind a tree trunk. Then she spotted another – and another. "Look!"

Twenty Icicle Imps scurried out and closed in around them in a circle. They didn't look nearly so cute now that Sophie knew how vicious they were.

"What are we going to do, Soph?" Sam said, as they edged together.

"Escape?" suggested Sophie.

"Great idea. How?"

"I'm still working on that part of the plan," admitted Sophie.

"Give us the gem," squeaked one of the Icicle Imps with a scowl.

"We haven't got a gem," bluffed Sophie, horribly aware of the belt she was wearing around her waist with the four gems inside it.

"We know you went to find one. We heard you talking about it."

Sophie's heart sank. The imps must have really excellent hearing. "We didn't find it," she told him.

"I think you lie!" exclaimed the Icicle Imp. He leapt straight at her face. Her Guardian powers tingling, Sophie moved in a blur of speed, kicking out high in the air and catching the Icicle Imp full on the chin. He bounced away, but the other imps were already jumping at her and Sam.

"Here, Soph! Use this!" Sam thrust the thermos of hot chocolate into her hands.

"Take that, you crazy ice balls!" Sophie gasped. She splattered hot chocolate everywhere. She expected the imps to howl and run away or even start melting maybe, but nothing happened! The drops of hot chocolate froze as they came into contact with the imps' icy fur. The imps shook themselves and the droplets flew off like little brown hailstones.

"Ha! You don't think we can be hurt by heat, do you?" scoffed the leader. "Our fur is

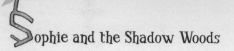

so cold that hot liquid will just freeze if it hits us! And if you try and attack us with heat we can throw invisible icy barriers around ourselves for protection." He whipped an icicle from his fur and held it like a spear. "You cannot hurt us, Guardian!"

"Maybe not, but I can get away from you!" Grabbing Sam, Sophie raced off with him up the bridle path, reaching the end in just the blink of an eye and dumping him on the edge of the village green. She swung round, but to her relief felt her powers fading. The imps must have decided not to follow them.

"Phew!" she said. "They've gone. I feel normal again."

Sam made a face. "It's getting embarrassing being rescued like this by you all the time."

"Forget about being embarrassed," Sophie replied. "Think of some way we can fight the imps! If we can't use heat to hurt them, what can we do?"

Sam sighed. "I think we'd better go back to yours and make another plan."

Mrs B's friends were all in the kitchen when Sophie and Sam got back. They were helping package everything up and price things for the next day at the fête. Sophie could hear their brisk, practical voices coming from the kitchen.

"Could someone pass me the greaseproof paper, please?"

"Shall we say eight or ten biscuits for a pound?"

Sophie and Sam went up to Sophie's bedroom and flopped on the bed.

"OK, so we've got two problems," Sam announced. "The first is how are we going to fight the Icicle Imps and stop them spying on us? The second is where is the diamond gem?"

Sophie sat bolt upright as tingles swept through her. "Oh, no! My powers! There must be an Icicle Imp nearby again!"

They ran to the window, but there was nothing to be seen. They went to the landing and checked the windows there, opening them and peering out.

"What are you two doing?" Anthony said, coming out of his bedroom.

"Nothing," Sophie told him distractedly. She didn't have time for Anthony just then.

"Do you want to know a secret?" The words burst out of Anthony. For once, he sounded properly excited.

It was so unlike him that Sophie turned. "What secret?"

"Come into my room!" Anthony said gleefully.

Sophie almost dropped through the floor. Anthony never asked her into his room.

"Come on!" he urged, beckoning them in.

Sophie and Sam went to his bedroom door.

"There!" Anthony pointed triumphantly across the room to where the old hamster cage from the garage was now sitting on his desk. "I've got a pet!"

Sophie stared. In the hamster cage was an Icicle Imp!

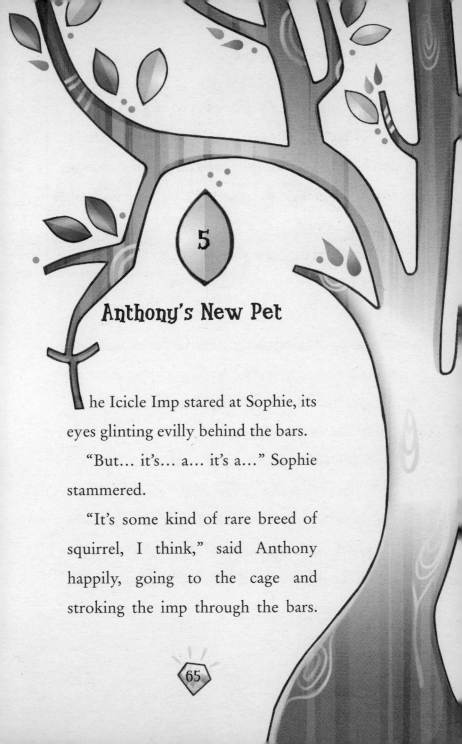

5

Anthony's New Pet

The Icicle Imp stared at Sophie, its eyes glinting evilly behind the bars.

"But… it's… a… it's a…" Sophie stammered.

"It's some kind of rare breed of squirrel, I think," said Anthony happily, going to the cage and stroking the imp through the bars.

65

"I was putting my bike away in the garage, and when I turned round he was just sitting there on the ground. He let me pick him up. He's really tame. Aren't you, Snowy?"

"Snowy?" Sophie echoed weakly.

"That's what I'm calling him," Anthony said, taking the imp out and cuddling him. "You love Daddy, don't you, Snowy?" The imp's fluffy face leered mockingly at Sophie and Sam from under Anthony's arm.

"But what will Mrs B say?" Sam asked, finding his voice at last.

"I'm not going to tell her just yet. I'm going to hide him and enter him in the pet show. I'll think of a way of getting her to let me keep him afterwards." The imp scampered up Anthony's arm and perched on his shoulder as Anthony walked over to his desk. "I've got an entry form right here."

"Anthony, you can't enter that thing in the show. You—"

Sophie broke off as Snowy pulled an icicle from its fur and threw it at Sam! Sophie reacted with superspeed, leaping in front of Sam and catching the icicle spear in mid-air.

Anthony looked round as she landed. "What are you doing?"

"It just attacked Sam!" Sophie exclaimed, as

the icicle melted in her hand.

Anthony stared. "Um, right. He's been on my shoulder the whole time."

The imp gave Sophie a triumphant smile, showing just the tips of its fangs, and then it nestled against Anthony's hair. Sophie felt a wave of horror. She had no doubt at all that it would be perfectly capable of managing to get in and out of its cage whenever it wanted to. She, Sam and Grandpa wouldn't be able to talk about anything to do with the gems or shadow creatures while it was in the house, probably creeping around and listening to their every word. An awful thought struck her. What if it discovered that she kept the four gems they had found already around her waist...?

"Anthony, you can't keep it!" Sophie burst out.

Anthony put the imp down on the bed. "Oh, really?"

"No!" Sophie strode grimly towards him.

Anthony stepped in front of Snowy. "Hands off!"

Sophie hesitated, anxious about overpowering Anthony when she was super-strong. She might really hurt him. "I'll... I'll tell Mrs B you've got a pet!" she threatened.

"Yeah! Then she'll make you get rid of it, Anthony!" Sam added.

"If you tell Mrs B about Snowy I'll tell her about all the times you two sneak off into the woods together," Anthony retorted. "You know we're not allowed to go in there. She'll ground you for life if she finds out, Sophie, and she'll stop Sam coming around!"

Sophie hesitated. It wasn't just the thought of

being grounded; she had suddenly realised she couldn't risk Mrs B seeing the imp in case the imp showed its fangs or spoke to her. Grandpa had often told her no one must ever find out shadow creatures existed.

While she was hesitating, the Icicle Imp leapt off the bed. "Grab it!" Sophie gasped.

Sam threw himself down, but the imp was faster and it dashed out through the open door!

"Snowy! Come back!" yelled Anthony.

They all scrambled to the doorway just in time to see the imp race down the stairs.

Sophie clapped her hands to her mouth. "What if Mrs B and her friends see it? We've got to get it back!"

They all charged after the imp. But by the time they reached the hall, Snowy had vanished.

"Where can it have gone?" Sam hissed.

Sophie ran into the lounge. Everywhere was
neat and tidy, the shelves and ornaments dusted,
the coffee table set up with plates ready for Mrs
B and her friends to have a cup of tea when they
finished preparing for the fête. Her skin tingled.
The air was very cold and she could see an icicle
hanging from the curtain pole.

"I think it's in here," she hissed to the boys.
"Quick! Get looking!"

Sam lifted the bottom of the curtains up
and shook them out. Sophie checked under the
table.

"Snowy? Little Snowy!" Anthony cooed,
crawling behind the sofa. "Come to Daddy."

"There!" Sam gasped, as the imp scurried up
the curtains. It reached the top of the curtain
rail and stared down at them like an evil, furry

gargoyle. Sam grabbed the metal poker from beside the fireplace and started jumping up and down, trying to knock the imp off.

"Don't hurt my Snowy!" Anthony howled, throwing himself over the sofa and landing with a crash on the floor.

Sophie started forwards to help Sam, but paused in horror at the sound of the kitchen door opening. "Come along, ladies!" Mrs B's cheerful voice rang out. "Our work's all done. Why don't you sit down in the lounge and I'll make us all a cup of tea?"

"Sam, stop!" hissed Sophie.

He didn't seem to hear. He was still leaping madly, waving the poker. "Come down, you fluffy ice ball!"

Mrs B and her three friends came into the room. They stopped and gaped in astonishment

at Anthony on the floor and Sam jumping up and down with a poker. One of Mrs B's friends gasped and put a hand to her mouth. Another gave a little shriek.

"Whatever is going on?" exclaimed Mrs B, her eyes bulging.

Sam froze.

"Sam's er... just doing a dance... a poker dance," Sophie gabbled.

"We've been learning it at school!" Anthony put in quickly, scrambling to his feet. "I was trying to do it too, but... I fell."

"A dance?" echoed Mrs B.

"Um... yes," said Sam. "It goes like this." Fixing a smile on his face he jumped to the left and then to the right, waving the poker over his head. "Dum de dum de dum de dum..."

From the corner of her eye, Sophie caught

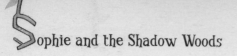

sight of something white dash past the ladies' feet. Luckily they were all too busy staring incredulously at Sam.

"Dum de... dum..." he finished weakly.

"Right." Mrs B cleared her throat. "Well, I think that's probably enough of your poker dance, Sam. It looks rather dangerous to me." She turned and smiled reassuringly at her friends. "Do sit down. I'm sorry it's so cold; I must get

Bob to have a look at the heating." She turned to Sophie, Sam and Anthony. "Now, out you go. Go on!" she said, shooing them away.

"But…" Anthony started to protest.

"No, it's OK," said Sophie. "Come on! Let's go!"

She dragged him out of the room. "I saw it leave," she whispered. "Though goodness knows where it's gone now."

There was a crash from the kitchen. They all stared at each other in dismay.

"Oh, no!" Sophie whispered. "Mrs B's cakes!"

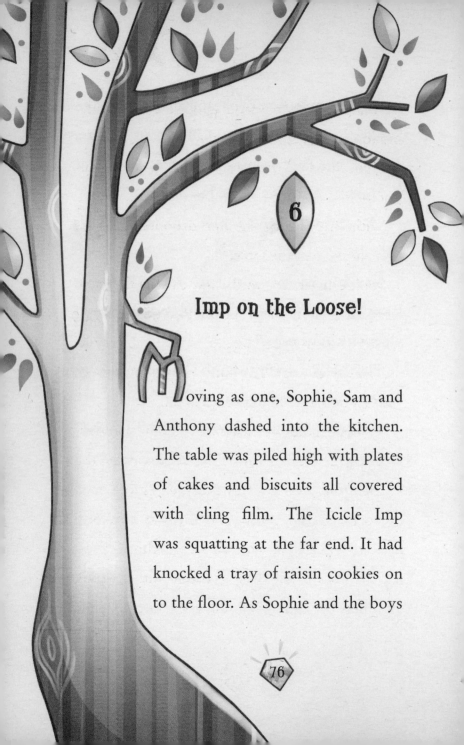

6

Imp on the Loose!

Moving as one, Sophie, Sam and Anthony dashed into the kitchen. The table was piled high with plates of cakes and biscuits all covered with cling film. The Icicle Imp was squatting at the far end. It had knocked a tray of raisin cookies on to the floor. As Sophie and the boys

ran in, it picked up a large chocolate fudge cake and looked at them tauntingly.

"No, Snowy!" Anthony cried. "Daddy will be cross!"

With an evil grin, the imp dropped the cake over the edge of the table.

Sophie dived forwards and caught the cake just as it was about to hit the floor. She sat up, the cake safe in her hands.

"Way to go, sis!" Anthony looked impressed.

"Get Snowy!" Sophie exclaimed.

Sam and Anthony leapt at the imp together. Hopping down from the table, he shot across the kitchen with the boys in pursuit. He bounced on to the work surface and then, as Anthony tried to grab him, jumped down through his legs. Anthony fell over, crashing into a stool. Cackling, the imp dived under the kitchen table with Sam following it.

"What in heaven's name is going on now?" Mrs B said as she came into the kitchen. She stared at Anthony who was tangled up with the stool, and then at Sophie who was holding the chocolate cake in her hands.

Sophie saw the imp scurry past Mrs B into the hall. "Quick!" she shrieked. "Into the hall."

"Oh, no!" snapped Mrs B, shutting the door behind her. "You two are going nowhere! Sophie, what are you doing with that cake?"

Sophie bit her lip. "It um... it fell off the table."

Mrs B's eyebrows rose. "Cakes do not just fall off tables. Neither do biscuits!" she said crossly, as she looked at the raisin cookies on the floor. "What are you thinking of, playing games in the kitchen like this? And where's Sam?"

"Here, Mrs B." Sam crawled sheepishly out from under the table.

Sophie thought Mrs B was going to explode like a volcano. "Right. That's it! Out! All of you! I don't want to see you in the kitchen again until teatime. OUT!"

They left the kitchen with her cross voice still ringing in their ears. "Wow, is she mad with us!" said Anthony.

"I can't say I blame her," muttered Sophie.

"And we still haven't got Snowy," groaned Sam.

"We'll keep looking," said Sophie determinedly.

But although they hunted high and low there was no sign of the Icicle Imp anywhere. A little while later, Grandpa came back. Leaving Anthony still searching, Sophie and Sam dragged Grandpa up to his bedroom. "You mean to say you let an Icicle Imp loose in the house?"

"We didn't exactly 'let it loose'; it escaped!" Sophie said.

Grandpa ran a hand over his hair. "But you know no one must find out about the shadow

creatures, Sophie. As Guardian it is your duty to keep the Shadow Realm secret. People cannot know about it – they would be terrified if they knew shadow creatures really did exist in our world. No one would sleep soundly in their beds at night. There would be panic. It must not happen."

"It's not my fault the imp's escaped and is somewhere in the house," Sophie protested. "Anthony found it. Still, at least it's only him who's seen it so far, and he thinks it's some kind of squirrel."

"But has it left the house yet? Can you feel your powers still?"

"Um... yes," Sophie admitted.

"So, it must be somewhere here still. At any moment Mrs B could meet it!" Grandpa paced up and down. "This is a disaster waiting to

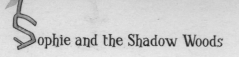

happen and it's all because you rushed in without thinking once again. Instead of threatening to throw the imp out, you should have just left well enough alone until I got back. Then I could have told Anthony he couldn't keep a pet and confiscated the cage with the imp in it. That would have been what a sensible person would have done."

He glared.

Sophie went red. Put like that, she had to agree with him. "I'm… I'm sorry, Grandpa."

"Unfortunately 'sorry' won't solve this mess! When will you learn to be more sensible?" Grandpa groaned. "Get looking for that imp and don't stop until you find it!"

However, Snowy was not to be found. Sophie went to bed that night feeling very on edge. She

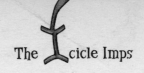

knew the imp was still in the house; there were patches of frost everywhere and her Guardian powers were tingling. She lay in bed, tensing up at every tiny sound. What if the Icicle Imp crept into her room during the night? She was wearing the gems around her waist under her pyjamas. She folded her arms over the pouch and hugged it to her.

She didn't sleep well at all.

The next morning she got up later than usual and went downstairs for breakfast, yawning and bleary-eyed.

Mrs B was in full-on organising mood, overseeing Anthony as he carried the cakes out to the car. Sophie was surprised to see her brother looking happy and helping. She thought he'd still be miserable about losing Snowy, but

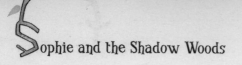

he looked remarkably cheerful.

"Where's Grandpa?" Sophie asked, as she helped herself to some cereal.

"He's gone on ahead to the village green to help get the tents set up and make sure the paths aren't too slippery with all this ice around," replied Mrs B. "Chop-chop, Sophie. I need you to get dressed and help me get the spare crockery out of the garage. It's so chilly today, I'm sure there are going to be lots of people wanting a cup of tea."

Sophie quickly ate her breakfast. Going upstairs again, she was relieved to find that her Guardian powers had faded. Maybe that meant the Icicle Imp had finally left the house!

She got dressed. She and Sam had agreed to meet at the fête at 10 a.m. *I hope we don't have to stay long*, she thought. We've got to try and find

the diamond gem as soon as possible.

As Sophie went outside, she felt her powers start up again. So the Icicle Imp was still nearby, just not in the house. Keeping a careful eye out, she helped Mrs B and Anthony load the boxes of crockery into the car. She had to remember to act as if they were heavy, when with her superstrength she really could have lifted all of them in one go!

The garage had been converted from an old outbuilding a while ago and it still had old-fashioned beams inside. Sophie looked upwards uneasily. She could just imagine the fluffy Icicle Imp sitting on a beam watching her, but there was no sign of it.

Sophie's eyes fell on a piece of old wood nailed between two of the walls in one of the far corners. She frowned. What was that? It reminded her of something she'd seen recently...

"Just a few more boxes!" declared Mrs B, patting her shoulder as she passed. "Come on now!"

Sophie pushed away the thought and helped Anthony shift the last couple of boxes, then it was time to go. They got into the car. As Sophie sat down, her powers surged through her so strongly she felt like she was on fire. She squeaked.

"Are you all right, duckie?" Mrs B said, looking around from the driver's seat.

"Y... yes," Sophie stammered. She glanced behind her wildly. Even the ends of her hair were tingling. The Icicle Imp had to be really close by. Maybe it was on the car roof or something!

Mrs B started the engine.

Anthony gave Sophie a curious glance.

"What's up?"

"Nothing," she said in a low voice as Mrs B started to drive. "What about you though? I thought you'd be more upset with Snowy having vanished."

Anthony grinned. "Ah, but he hasn't vanished!" He lifted a towel covering a rectangular shape at his feet and Sophie gasped.

Under the towel was the cage with the Icicle Imp inside!

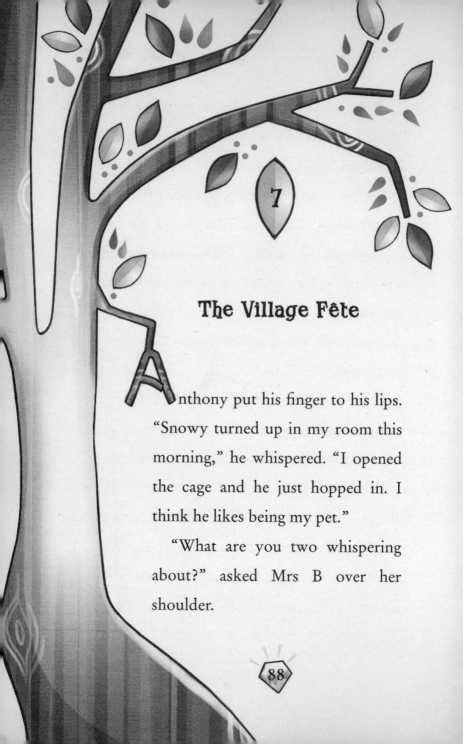

7

The Village Fête

Anthony put his finger to his lips. "Snowy turned up in my room this morning," he whispered. "I opened the cage and he just hopped in. I think he likes being my pet."

"What are you two whispering about?" asked Mrs B over her shoulder.

"I was just saying I hope the fête goes well, Mrs B, and you sell lots of cakes," Anthony said innocently.

Sophie couldn't take her eyes off the imp. As Anthony chatted to Mrs B, the little white creature pulled an icicle from behind its left ear and flung it viciously at Sophie's ankle. "Ow!" she yelped.

Anthony looked around in surprise.

"What's the matter, duckie?" Mrs B asked.

"N... nothing." Sophie rubbed her ankle and glared at the imp who just grinned at her, showing a flash of its fangs. She yanked the cover back down over it. For a moment she wondered about telling Mrs B and getting her to stop the car. But what could she say? She remembered Grandpa's warning. No one must ever find out about the shadow creatures.

Be sensible, she told herself, her thoughts racing. She would wait until they got to the fête and then tell Grandpa and let him decide what to do. At least it wasn't far to the green.

"Brr," said Mrs B. "The car heater doesn't seem to be working very well today. I don't know what's happening to the weather at the moment! The sun's shining and feels hot, but everywhere is so icy still. I've never known anything like it." She tutted. "It must be global warming."

As soon as Mrs B had parked, Anthony jumped out with the hamster cage still covered by the old towel. "I'll be back in a minute – I've just got to do something," he said, as Mrs B started opening the car boot.

"Anthony, come back!" the housekeeper called, but he was already hurrying towards the main marquee.

Sophie knew exactly what her brother was doing. He was about to enter the Icicle Imp in the pet show! She had to stop him before the show started and people saw Snowy's fangs! *I've got to find Grandpa*, she thought desperately.

"I'm just going to… have a look around," she said, taking a step backwards.

"Oh, no you don't. Your brother's disappeared, you're not going to too," said Mrs B firmly, plonking a box of plates into Sophie's arms. "You can help me unload the car first."

Sophie carried the plates to the marquee as fast as she could. Maybe Grandpa would be there? Someone had spread rock salt on the icy ground, and it crunched under her feet.

"Hi!" Sam came jogging over as she reached the tent. He lowered his voice. "Any sign of the Icicle Imp?"

In a whisper, Sophie told him everything. "I have to find Grandpa and see if he can get Snowy away from Anthony before the pet show starts! Do you know where he is?"

Sam shook his head. "No, I haven't seen him."

"Hi, you two."

They looked around. Daisy was riding past on Blue.

"Hi, Daisy!" Sam and Sophie called distractedly.

Daisy waved and rode on. As she did so, a picture flashed into Sophie's mind – the strange wooden shape in the corner of her garage. Suddenly she made the connection. The last time she had seen something like that had been the manger in the corner of Blue's stable!

Her eyes widened, thoughts clicking into place in her head. Her garage at home was old. What if it had once been a stable? Mrs B would know.

"Sam! Quick! I've got to talk to Mrs B about something!" She dumped the plates in his arms. "I'll meet you in the tent. Keep an eye on Anthony and try to find Grandpa then tell him about the imp! I'll be back in a sec!"

Before Sam could answer, Sophie was racing back to the car. Mrs B was still sorting things out. "Mrs B! Our garage!" The words burst out of Sophie. "Was it once a stable?"

"Yes, duckie." Mrs B looked surprised. "It was built about the same time as the cottage. Your parents converted it into a garage about fifteen years ago. Why?"

"Oh, no reason." Sophie's mind whirled. Of course! The clue talked about where ponies and horses had slept for the night. Not where they slept now. The garage had once been a stable and it had a gable window. Maybe the diamond gem was hidden in there! *We've got to get back and check*, she thought.

"Here are some more plates," said Mrs B, loading her up again.

Sophie hurried back to the tent. There was one long table full of cut flowers for the best blooms competition. Exhibitors were fussing around, trying to make their displays look the best. Lots of ladies were bustling by the refreshment table,

setting out teacups and cakes. They all had smart dresses on and were wearing hats. The Lady Mayoress was there too – her hat was easily the largest, a saucer-like creation trimmed with plastic cherries. There was a cheerful atmosphere as everyone greeted each other and helped out.

"Hello, Sophie!" called Mr Badgett, Grandpa's friend and Daisy's grandfather, who owned the local junk shop. He was carrying a beautiful bunch of orange chrysanthemums.

"Hi, Mr Badgett. Have you seen Grandpa?" Sophie asked quickly.

"I just saw him a few moments ago, checking the guy ropes on the tent," answered Mr Badgett. "Your grandpa's always so sensible and safety-conscious."

"Thanks."

Sophie caught sight of Sam hovering anxiously

as Anthony set up Snowy's cage next to a girl who had brought her hamster along with a pink bow tied around its neck. To Sophie's relief, the towel was still covering Snowy's cage. She dumped the plates on the table and ran over to Sam. "Quick! Mr Badgett says Grandpa's outside, and I think I know where the gem is! It's—" She broke off as she suddenly realised that the Icicle Imp would no doubt be able to hear every word she was saying from its cage!

"What?" said Sam, frowning.

But it was too late, the imp had heard! It hooked its arm through the bars, under the cloth and opened the cage. Letting itself out, it streaked across the tent towards Sophie.

"My squirrel's escaped!" yelled Anthony.

Elderly ladies in their best hats squealed as the Icicle Imp darted around their stockinged

legs. Mr Badgett tried to dive and grab it, but it leapt out of his way. It landed on the flower table and charged along it, knocking over vases and sending brightly coloured flowers flying in all directions, a wicked leer on its face. The flower exhibitors all yelled.

best bloom

"My beautiful roses!"

"My perfect geraniums!"

Hands grabbed for the Icicle Imp, but it was too fast. It leapt off the table and landed on the Lady Mayoress's hat!

"Ah!" she shrieked, her blonde curls wobbling. The Icicle Imp hung down and looked her straight in the eyes. The Lady Mayoress shrieked

and fainted into the arms of the man beside her. Then the imp leapt down to the ground and galloped away.

"Stop that animal!" yelled everyone around her, as the imp darted through people's legs towards Sophie and Sam.

Thoughts rushed through Sophie's head. What could they do now? They had to get away and look for the gem, but they also had to stop anyone seeing the Icicle Imp's fangs or hearing it talk. Suddenly she had an idea. "The gem's here in the tent, Sam!" she yelled as loudly as she could. "Quick, find it!"

"What?" Sam gaped, as if she'd gone mad.

"Not really," Sophie hissed directly into his ear. "It's just we've got to get out of here without Snowy following us or showing anyone it's a shadow creature. We need to distract it!" She looked to see if her plan had worked. It had! Instead of heading towards her the Icicle Imp had turned round and was now frantically whizzing across the tent, looking under tables, checking inside flower pots, jumping from cage to cage on the pet table and sending all the animals wild as it searched around them with its long fingers. The shouting and screaming grew louder.

"Let's go!" Grabbing Sam's hand, Sophie pulled him to the door. As they reached the entrance they collided with Grandpa who was striding inside. "What's going on?" he demanded.

"Anthony's Icicle Imp's loose in there!" Sophie whispered. "It thinks the gem is in the tent. Sam and I think it's back at home though. We need to get away."

"And you need to catch the imp!" said Sam.

Grandpa looked at the bedlam in front of him

and gave a nod. "No problem. I know how I can help with both those things."

He strode back out of the tent. Sophie and Sam ran after him. "What are you doing, Grandpa?" Sophie demanded.

"This!" Taking a penknife out of his pocket, Grandpa cut through one of the ropes holding the tent up. Sophie and Sam watched open-mouthed as he ran around the tent and cut through the next rope and the next. The tent started to billow and then suddenly collapsed! Everyone inside shrieked and yelled.

Grandpa looked at Sam and Sophie. "Explain later! Go!"

They didn't need telling twice. They turned and ran!

Sophie and Sam charged across the green. Sophie

wondered about using her superspeed, but now they were away from the tent she could feel her powers fading. She let out a relieved breath. "I don't think it's following us," she said to Sam.

When they reached her house, the main door at the back of the garage under the gable was locked, but the side door was open. They turned on the light and Sophie whispered the clue:

"Where ponies and horses slept for the night
Look in the gable, the gem is in sight."

Her eyes went upwards to the round window in the gable. It had a wide window ledge. Maybe the gem was up there somewhere? But how was she going to get up there to search?

Sam dragged out an old stool and a chest. "Try climbing up these," he said, putting the stool on top of the chest. But though it made Sophie higher, she still couldn't get her hands

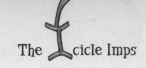

anywhere near the ledge. "I need to get closer," she exclaimed in frustration.

Suddenly she felt a tingling in her toes. She turned to Sam. "The Icicle Imp must be coming. I can feel my powers!"

"We've got to get the gem before it gets here," Sam said frantically.

Sophie looked at the window and realised that with her Guardian powers it would be no problem at all! Bending her knees, she jumped, springing all the way up and grabbing the ledge with her fingers. She wriggled and pulled herself up on to it, sneezing as clouds of dust flew up. It was a squeeze, but she could just about fit on. She looked around. There! Nestling in one corner was a dusty gem. She grabbed it and rubbed it on her t-shirt. It sparkled like a big diamond!

103

"I've got it, Sam!" She jumped down all the way to the ground, landing nimbly. She showed him the gem in delight.

"Brilliant! Put it with the others!" he urged. "And then let's get out of here before the Icicle Imps realise what we're doing and where we are."

Sophie tucked it into the pouch with the other gems. It clinked softly against them. "Five down, just one more to get!" she said in delight.

"Let's go!" said Sam, eyeing the door nervously.

Sophie strode over. With her powers coursing through her she didn't feel scared at all. So what if Snowy was out there. He was just one imp. She could fight him!

"Come on, Snowy – bring it on!" she muttered, as she flung open the door.

But what she saw took her breath away. Hundreds of Icicle Imps were marching down the driveway towards her, their eyes fixed on the garage, sharp icicles in their bony fingers and their pointed fangs gleaming...

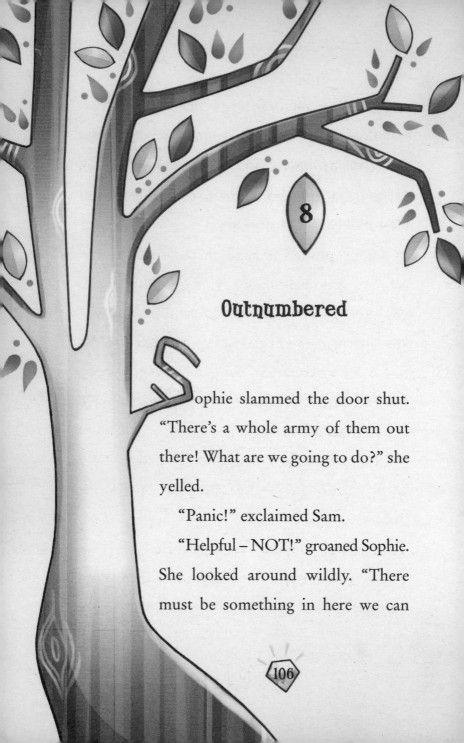

8

Outnumbered

Sophie slammed the door shut. "There's a whole army of them out there! What are we going to do?" she yelled.

"Panic!" exclaimed Sam.

"Helpful – NOT!" groaned Sophie. She looked around wildly. "There must be something in here we can

use to fight them with."

There were the empty shelves where the crockery had been, old bikes, a few bits of furniture, a sink and a hosepipe. Nothing much else.

Sophie pushed a hand through her fringe. There was no way they'd be able to battle their way out past all those Icicle Imps. But they couldn't just stay in the garage. She felt a shiver of horror as she imagined Mrs B coming back from the fête and seeing all the imps there. She'd have a heart attack!

Maybe there was some way she could fight her way through? Sophie cautiously opened the door.

"Get her!" shrieked a savage voice.

Two of the Icicle Imps leapt at her face, their fangs glinting. Sophie reacted instinctively, batting them down with her fists. They fell to her feet and she kicked them away, even though she knew they'd just be back again in a second. But to her amazement, instead of bouncing harmlessly, the imps screeched and started to fizzle and melt into puddles.

"Sophie! Watch out!" Sam yelled, as the other Icicle Imps all started to throw their icicles at her. He pulled her inside and slammed the door. A second later a hundred icicles battered against the wood like tiny frozen arrows.

"If you'd still been out there you'd have been really hurt!" Sam cried. "Don't go out again!" The door started to move as the imps reached it and tried to push it open.

Sophie didn't argue. She flung herself against the door, using all her strength to keep it shut.

"We heard you talking to your grandfather and saying the gem was back here," squeaked the leader. "It's ours now!"

"We want the gem! We want the gem!" the rest of the imps shrieked together like manic sabre-toothed toddlers.

Sophie could feel the imps battering the door, pushing at it. "Sam, did you see what happened to those two imps I kicked?" she yelled above the row outside. "They melted! I kicked them and they started to dissolve. Why?"

Sam had thrown his weight against the door too. "I don't know," he panted. "It didn't happen last time you fought the imps, so there's got to be something different today. Are you wearing different shoes?"

"No, I've just got my trainers on, same as always," said Sophie.

They looked at her feet.

"There!" Sam yelled, making Sophie almost leap in the air.

"What? Where?"

Sam pointed at her trainers. The toes were encrusted with an orangey-brown grit. "You've got rock salt on them – it was on the paths at the fête and there's some stuck on your shoes. Why didn't I think of it before? Salt melts ice! I knew that! People put it on paths to melt ice and snow. It must work on Icicle Imps too!"

"Brilliant!" gasped Sophie and then her expression fell. "But how does that help us? We haven't got much on our shoes. Not enough to fight all those imps out there."

"Oh, if only we had some more," groaned Sam.

"Wait – there's some in the shed!" exclaimed Sophie, remembering how Mrs B had sent Grandpa to get a bag from there the day before.

"Brilliant. Pity there's an army of Icicle Imps

between us and it," Sam said. "There's no way we can fight our way through all of them to get there."

"I wish we could just freeze them in place and run and get it," Sophie said desperately. Outside, the imps were still howling loudly as they pushed at the door. At least they wouldn't hear what was being said, thought Sophie. They were too busy shrieking for the gem!

"Hang on." Sam looked at the sink and the hose, then back at her, his eyes suddenly shining. "Maybe that's not such an impossible idea."

"What do you mean?" she demanded. "How can we freeze them? They freeze everything they touch!"

"Exactly," said Sam. "They're so cold that if we put water on top of them it will freeze." He ran to the hosepipe, excitement on his face.

"Don't you see what that means? If we spray loads of water on them with the hose, they'll freeze it and then they'll be stuck inside a wall of ice!"

Sophie blinked as she struggled to hold the door on her own. "You really think that will work?"

"It's the only hope we've got," said Sam.

Sophie lifted her chin. "Then let's do it!"

"We'll have to be quick," Sam instructed. "You open the door and I'll spray them." He turned the tap on. Water jetted out of the hosepipe, bouncing around the garage. "Ready?" he cried.

"Ready!" said Sophie, taking hold of the door handle and bracing herself. "One, two, three..."

"It's chill-out time!" yelled Sam, as Sophie opened the door. He shoved the nozzle of the hose out and sprayed water full blast over the

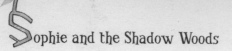

front row of imps. They screeched in surprise and anger. They started leaping for the crack in the door, but as the water covered them, they froze it – and turned immediately into little blocks of ice! The imps could still be seen inside the blocks, their cute faces twisted into furious savage expressions, but they couldn't move. They were stuck, like a row of ice cubes, sparkling in the sun.

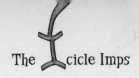

The imps behind screamed in fury and threw their icicles straight at Sam and Sophie's heads.

"Be careful, Sam!" Sophie gasped, yanking Sam down to the ground just in time. "Stay down!"

Grabbing the hosepipe from him, she darted towards the imps at the back. Using her superspeed, she jumped over the blocks of ice, dodging and ducking round the flying icicles at the same time. She charged at the imps at the back, the water spraying from the hose. "Watch out, ice balls. Here I come!" she yelled.

"Go, Sophie!" Sam whooped.

The water sprayed all over the back rows of imps. With shrieks they started to turn to ice too.

Silence suddenly fell. After all the screeching and screaming it sounded eerily quiet. Sophie looked around, tense, waiting for a surprise attack. But every single imp was now frozen in place.

"We did it!" she said, stunned.

Sam scrambled to his feet. "Quick, let's get the rock salt! If Mrs B comes back and sees all the

imps like this, she won't believe for a second that they're just squirrels!"

Sophie grinned. "I bet she'd scream loud enough to break the ice!"

They ran to the shed. There were ten bags of rock salt there. They were very heavy, but Sophie could pick them up easily – her superstrength hadn't dimmed even though the imps were frozen. "You know, it feels a bit mean, just melting them while they're all stuck," she said, walking back to the garage and looking around at the imp ice cubes.

"Mean?" Sam echoed. "Sophie, these are Icicle Imps! They were trying to attack us and get the gem!"

Then there was a faint cracking sound, and then another and another.

"What's that noise?" asked Sophie slowly.

Sam's eyes widened and he glanced up. "The sun! It's melting the ice!" The cracking grew louder. "Sophie, do something! They're about to break free!"

As Sophie watched, the imps started to fight free of the blocks, their small hands clawing their way out, their fangs ripping through the ice. A tiny icicle hit Sam's cheek leaving a bloody mark.

"Attack the humans!" screeched a voice. "Show no mercy!"

Sophie gave up trying to be nice. Ripping open the bag of salt, she raced towards the imps and chucked it all over them, as a shower of icicles fell around her. Sam had dragged another bag out of the shed and was flinging handfuls everywhere. The imps screeched, melting and dissolving or turning and running away.

"Noooooo!" howled the leader, as he shrank

away to nothing. "The gem was ours, ours, ou—!" His voice became a glub as he turned to water.

In less than a minute, the driveway was clear, covered with pools of water and piles of brown grit. Breathing hard, Sophie and Sam looked around.

"We've done it," said Sam in relief. "This time the imps really have gone!"

Sophie met his hand in a high five. "Way to go, us!"

"Yeah, defeating Icicle Imps – what's the problem? It's no big deal," said Sam with a grin.

A thought struck Sophie. "The fête might be a big deal though, after Grandpa collapsed the tent! I wonder what's happening there – and if anyone has found out that Snowy's a shadow creature yet! Oh, I hope not!"

Sam gulped. "Guess we'd better go back and find out."

9

Saving the Day

Sophie and Sam raced back to the village green. When they got there they found the tent being put back up and the tables set out again. Mrs B was talking to Anthony and Grandpa. Anthony had the empty cage in his hands.

"Anthony, how could you have

smuggled a strange animal in like that and cause so much chaos?" Mrs B was saying helplessly. "What were you thinking? It was clearly wild and shouldn't have been in a cage!"

Anthony hung his head. "Sorry, Mrs B."

"And I just can't understand how the tent collapsed like that," Mrs B went on to Grandpa. "So suddenly, with no warning!"

"I've got absolutely no idea," Grandpa said, spotting Sophie and giving her a wink.

"I guess it was just one of those things," Sophie put in.

Mrs B turned. "Sophie!" She looked relieved. "Where have you been? I was worried about you."

"Sam and I just popped home to fetch something," Sophie replied. This time it was her turn to wink at Grandpa.

"Did you get it?" he asked eagerly.

"Oh, yes. And we dealt with another problem while we were there, Grandpa."

"A very icy problem," Sam put in.

Grandpa looked delighted. "Excellent!"

"Well, there are plenty of problems here," sighed Mrs B. "I need to set up all over again in order to be able to serve tea."

"We'll help," Sophie offered. Sam nodded. Anthony still had his head down, staring glumly at the empty cage.

"Thank you, duckies," Mrs B said.

"I'll just go and put this cage by the car," Anthony sighed. "It's no use having a cage without a pet, and I saw Snowy run off into the trees. I guess he won't ever come back." He walked away slowly, his shoulders hunched over forlornly.

Sophie felt a rush of sympathy. Maybe she and Anthony didn't usually get along, but he'd been almost OK the last two days… and he'd really seemed to like Snowy. She turned impulsively to Mrs B. "Mrs B, couldn't Anthony have a pet? I don't mind. I won't ask for one. Just a hamster or a gerbil, nothing big."

"It would be fine by me," said Grandpa. "I'm sure their parents wouldn't mind."

Mrs B watched Anthony reach the car. "Well, a hamster would certainly be far less trouble than that squirrel creature he had today." She hesitated and glanced around at them all. "Oh, all right," she said, giving in. She hurried after Anthony. "Anthony! Wait!"

"Brilliant," Sophie smiled. "Anthony'll be happy now and hopefully it'll stop him trying to catch any other shadow creatures to keep as pets!"

"So, what's been going on? You found the gem then?" Grandpa said.

"Yes, it was in the garage and we also got rid of the Icicle Imps, Grandpa! Sam had a brilliant idea." She quickly told him all about it.

"Excellent work, both of you!" Grandpa beamed. "You know, sometimes I think there's hope for you yet."

Sophie decided to take that as praise. "Thanks for letting down the tent and giving us a chance to escape." Her eyes teased him. "Though maybe it wasn't the most sensible thing to do, Grandpa."

Grandpa's gaze met hers. "You know, the more time I spend with you, the more I'm beginning to think that sometimes being sensible isn't always the answer." He grinned and for a moment looked about ten years old too. "And it was lots of fun! Did you hear them all shriek?"

Sophie and Sam giggled. "Oh, yes!" Sam said.

"We really have to get the last gem now," Sophie put in. "Imagine if the gate opened and lots of other shadow creatures came out and into our world. It was bad enough with just Snowy here today. Think of what it would be like with thousands of shadow creatures."

They gave each other worried looks.

"We'll get the gem," said Grandpa determinedly.

Sam nodded. "Those shadow creatures won't stop us," he declared. "Snow way!"

Sophie smiled back. "Snow way at all!"

10

In the Woods...

Deep in the trees, Ug howled as he stared at the Icicle Imp in front of him. "What do you mean you're giving up?"

The Imp shook its head. "She's destroyed us. She has beaten us. We want nothing more to do with that Guardian."

"But I need a gem!"

"Then you will have to find someone else to get it, King Ug." The Icicle Imp turned and marched away.

Potato Nose sniggered as it passed him. "Not so scary, after all, are you?"

With an evil look, the Icicle Imp whipped an icicle from its fur and plunged it into Potato Nose's foot.

"Ow!" yelled Potato Nose.

As the Icicle Imp's fluffy white fur vanished into the trees, Ug thumped his throne in frustration. Now what was he going to do? It didn't seem to matter what he threw at the girl, she always managed to defeat him! And now there was only one gem left to find.

"It's time for some flying power," he muttered, jumping down from his throne. He smiled as he realised what he would do. Oh, yes. He lifted his flaking chin. One last gem. One last chance. This time he would not be defeated.

THE

SHADOW

FILES

Icicle Imps

Excellent hearing

BEWARE...

An Icicle Imp will bring freezing temperatures.

...FANGS!!!

Never ever follow an Icicle Imp into the woods.
One imp is bad. Lots of imps is VERY bad.
And never ever EVER keep an Icicle Imp as a pet!

Signs of Icicle Imps being close by:
Frost
Icicles everywhere
Freezing cold air

How do Icicle Imps like to travel? By bICICLE.

Snow Goblins

Brings snow wherever it goes.
Hibernates in summer.
Never seen between May and September.
Ice in summer? Refer to Shadow Files
on Icicle Imps...

Ideas for fighting snow and ice shadow creatures

Weapons:

hosepipe

sunlight (maybe)

rocksalt

hairdryer (maybe)

oven (hard to use, but possible)

Other Ideas:

Make them dance until they get so hot they melt?

Um, Sophie... are you sure???

Places in the Shadow Woods that we've found so far...

The Gate

Fog Boggart's Cave

You do NOT want to go in here!

N
W E
S

The Shadow Woods are bigger inside than they look from the outside and there are all sorts of unusual things in there...

Spider Gnome's Web
(Take a parrot!)

Grandpa

Waterfall

Look out for Icicle Imps!

Ambush alert!

Wait, some of this stuff has MOVED! How can you have a map when things don't stay still?!

NOTES

What's next in store for Sophie?

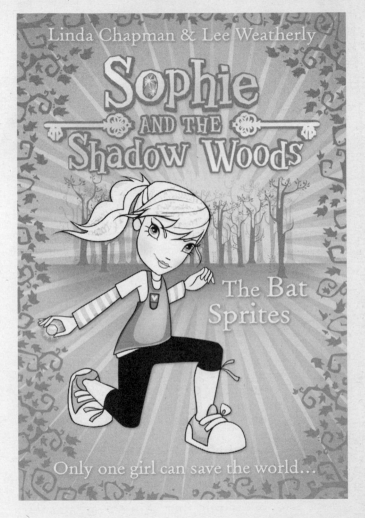

Turn the page
for a sneak peek...

he bat shrieked and grabbed at Sophie's foot with its long fingers, catching her ankle. Sophie saw its fangs flash down and managed to turn her fall into a back flip, yanking her foot free. She landed nimbly, dodging as the creature swung at her, and then kicked her leg out in a circle, her shin thwacking into the back of its legs. It fell forwards with a hiss.

"Oopsy, tripped again!" she grinned.

"Yeah, and take that!" Sam grabbed the bin and threw it over the creature's head. Balls of paper and apple cores rained out.

"Argh! Get this thing off me! Get it off!" The bat's voice was muffled as it staggered around, bumping into the bed and bookshelves. Its screeches and squeals echoed back to it until finally the bat toppled over and the bin fell off its head.

"You'll pay for that!" it screeched as it leapt at Sophie, yellow fangs bared. She snatched up a metal trophy she'd won for tae kwon do and thwacked it hard on its head.

The creature keeled over and lay still.

For a moment, there was silence. Sophie and Sam both stared at the bat's grey, furry body lying on the floor.

"Is it… is it… dead?" breathed Sam.

Sophie swallowed and bent over the creature. Its chest still seemed to be moving. She poked it with her foot, but it didn't stir. "I think I just knocked it out."

"Sophie!" Mrs B called up the stairs. "It sounds like there's a herd of elephants in your bedroom. What are you doing?"

Sophie ran to the door. "Nothing!" she called. She turned to Sam. "Quick! We've got to get rid of it!"

"Great idea! But how? It's as big as we are!"

"You must be up to something," Mrs B shouted. They heard her footsteps climbing the stairs.

Sophie looked wildly at Sam. "Oh, no! What do we do now?"

Sam's eyes were wide. "Panic!"

"Do you have what it takes to be the NEXT GUARDIAN?"

Prove your worth for a chance to win AWESOME prizes!
It's simple and fun!

Read the *Sophie and the Shadow Woods* series
Answer three questions about each book
Pass a stage, collect a gem, enter for great prizes/freebies
Pass SIX stages and get entered into the grand prize draw!

Stage Five

Answer these simple questions about *The Icicle Imps*:

1. What name does Anthony give his new 'pet'?
2. Where was the diamond gem hidden?
3. What did Sam and Sophie use to make the Icicle Imps melt?

Got the answers? Go to:
www.sophieandtheshadowwoods.com
and continue the journey!

Look out for the final stage in *The Bat Sprites*, out in October.

Good Luck!